A MYSTERY IN GLACIER NATIONAL PARK

Two students, a pup coyote and an unspeakable crime

Earl Hanson

CONTENTS

INTRODUCTION

In his extraordinary new novel, storyteller, outdoorsman and retired attorney Earl Hanson weaves a gripping story set amid the beauty and excitement of Glacier National Park.

The author worked as a United State Immigration officer each summer in and adjacent to Glacier National Park for three years while he attended Law School in Montana. He was able to spend these summers with his young family. All were touched by their experiences in the Park.

He hiked and explored this National Park as time would allow. He met bears on the trail. He watched mountain goats graze on the high rock cliffs, and he fished in the many creeks and lakes of the Park. His young son would trail along with him on fishing trips.

He was stirred by the forest and wildlife and spent much of his adult life hiking, fishing, and backpacking in the many mountain ranges of Montana.

He has explored the most remote areas of both Yellowstone National Park and Glacier National Park.

The forests and wilderness of Glacier Park gives this story its stage. Its story begins at a resort Lodge and R.V. Park.

PROLOGUE

Andrew and Haven are high school students spending their summer working at the resort, Glacier Haven Inn, owned and operated by their parents and located at the south edge of Glacier National Park.

Andrew and Haven have lived at the resort since they were small children.

The summer was soon going to be busy. Little did they know or expect how much excitement, drama and fear would face them in this unforgettable summer.

The work was difficult. They would clean rooms, change beds, do laundry, set tables, cook meals, and serve guests in many ways.

They kept the premises clean and pristine so they could enjoy the wilderness setting.

They always loved the break from their work, though, when they could hike for short distances. This day, they set out to explore the beautiful forest behind their Lodge. What would happen next would change their lives forever.

CHAPTER 1

A MOST UNEXPECTED GUEST

As they walked, they heard a whimper which sounded like a cry from a small animal. Andrew ran to investigate the sound.

Haven was right behind her brother. She came up to a little ball of fur.

Andrew cried out, “It looks like a small house cat curled into a ball!”

Haven said, “I have a sweatshirt; I will run and get it.”

She picked up the small whimpering animal and wrapped it in the sweatshirt.

The little animal turned out to be an infant coyote. The pup appeared to be only a few days or a week old. It was lying adjacent to the railroad track next to the property of the Lodge.

They noticed the coyote pup was severely injured. Blood was dripping from the right leg, and it was obvious the little limb was either badly out of joint or the leg was broken.

The baby coyote could hardly whimper loud enough to be heard.

Haven yelled, “Let see if the mother coyote is around!”

Just as she spoke, Andrew exclaimed, "Oh no! I have found his mother and she must have been hit by the train which passed through here about an hour ago. She didn't make it; let us search for any other babies in the area."

They searched the area and found no other baby coyotes. They hurried into action.

Andrew knew the basic Montana Law concerning baby wild animals found alone in the forest.

The law required the public to leave a wild baby alone and as they found it. Usually the mother will return and take care of the baby animal. If the baby animal is injured, call a Game Warden.

The dilemma they faced was whether to call the Game Warden now and have him come by and pick up the baby coyote, or rescue the baby coyote themselves and worry about the Warden later. The choice was easy for these two highschool children.

In this case, the tiny pup coyote had lost its mother and there was no way to rescue this pup without taking him under their control and nursing him back to health. If they wanted to save this baby orphan coyote, they must act quickly.

Andrew said, "Hurry let's take this little fellow to our large playhouse."

They kept the coyote pup a secret from everyone. They had to come up with some ideas of how to medically treat and protect this precious little wild animal.

CHAPTER 2

THE EMERGENCY ROOM

The small playhouse was a perfect place to set up the emergency room.

First, how do they feed the baby coyote?

They had no idea how to proceed. Both had handled many research projects in high school and were both computer literate. They took a few moments on their computers to research some medical and nutrition questions.

Andrew took over the responsibility of planning. He assigned himself with the task of figuring out how to legally keep this little coyote.

He assigned Haven the immediate task of finding out what nutrition or type of food was needed to save this baby coyote's life.

What does a baby coyote eat, how does it eat, and how would these young people organize answers before the little wild animal would die of shock and starvation?

Andrew said, "We will work on the legal problems later. We need to act quickly to save the little guy."

Andrew pulled items he would need from a large first aid kit kept in the garage.

Haven on the other hand found a hot water bottle and a small eye dropper. They had earlier determined the pup was no more than a week old, and they had no idea if it would or could eat.

But they knew they had to feed this baby!

If it had a mother, they reasoned, it would nurse. So, Haven decided to make a milk potion. She used an eye dropper to deliver the milk to the baby.

She mixed milk, cream and honey and put the mixture into a small bowl.

She also placed a hot water bottle filled with warm water, under a small blanket and then gently placed the little baby coyote on the blanket. This immediately calmed the little pup down.

She gently stroked its little head with her hand until the pup stopped quivering. The eyedropper was placed near its mouth, and a little drop of the milk potion appeared at its tip. The coyote pup licked the drop from the dropper again and again. Andrew and Haven were encouraged they might have figured out the feeding problem for the time being.

The eyedropper continued to create little drops of milk, and the pup continued to lick the drops until he fell asleep. The baby pup was warm, safe, and satisfied from his milk. Haven would now become his new mother.

Later, Andrew gave him a complete medical inspection.

Andrew confirmed that his little right front leg was broken, but he said, "I think I know just how to fix it!"

Andrew prepared a tiny splint and placed it carefully on the tiny leg. He then wrapped a thin piece of medical tape around the stent until it was securely in place.

He had read enough about medical treatment to a broken bone to give him an idea of what to do in this emergency.

After the splint was in place, he then used antiseptic to wash the area around the leg, in the area where it had been bleeding.

He thoughtfully noted, "I don't think we should do anything until we attend to the emergency first aid."

The decisions they were making for this little fellow were decisions of life and death. Both the medical decisions and the legal decisions were vital.

If the Montana Fish and Game Department discovered the orphan baby coyote was held by a private citizen, they would seize the pup and euthanize it because of their experience of what would be best for the orphan and what would be best for the public. The State simply did not have facilities to take care of a baby coyote.

Since the mother coyote was dead, Heather and Andrew believed the verdict for the pup would not be promising in the hands of a Fish and Game Warden.

Andrew whispered, "We will not call the Fish and Game Warden for now."

The rules of the Fish and Game Department were sound, but in this case Andrew and Haven believed this little pup should be treated as an exception to the harsh rule. They determined they would try to save this precious little fellow who was so helpless.

After the pup had finished another feeding of milk from the eye dropper and endured the setting of the broken front leg, it fell back to sleep.

Andrew researched and learned coyote mothers usually carry their young by the nape of their neck when moving them from den to den.

Probably this pup was in its mother's grip moving him to a new den when they were struck by the moving train. Obviously, the baby flew away from the train after impact. It was truly a miracle he was not killed at the same instant his mother was struck by the train.

CHAPTER 3

THE COYOTE PUP GETS A NAME

Now, for the next major project! They would have to name this little pup coyote.

Haven was delighted with the decision to name the baby coyote. She said, "I love this little guy already; let us give him a name he will be proud of."

It might sound simple to name a pet, but this was not just a "pet"—he was truly a fugitive from jurisdiction of the Montana Fish and Game, the Forest Service and all the Wardens and officers whose job it was to enforce the law.

He was also a wild animal, and the name could not be the same as a name for a domestic puppy.

The little guy had won their hearts. The caregivers of the coyote considered Cody, Rusty, Chief, Wylie, King, and many other appropriate names.

But since the little fellow was a fugitive and needed to remain in hiding, they finally agreed upon "Bandit." Their little fugitive would remain in hiding. No one was to know about him.

It was difficult for the young students to do their work at the resort and tend to the little pup. Its feeding schedule was constant. Every 30 minutes he would lick the eye dropper, and he loved being petted on his little head as he ate. But their care made it so Bandit was thriving and getting stronger, larger, and more active each day.

They gave him new toys every day, and he would run, throw them, chase them, and try to tear them apart.

He seemed to be in constant motion either running, jumping, or hiding in some little hidden spot in the playhouse.

Food, care, love, and attention is what Bandit needed most. And that is what he got from Andrew and Haven. The little Coyote started looking to them as his parents.

Love abounded in the little hiding place where they kept Bandit. The playhouse had walls, windows, lights, a heater, and a door. They used to play there when they were little, so it was insulated from the cold. But now it was hardly used. Its chairs and table were handy for feeding and caring for Bandit. Andrew and Haven could not imagine how much work and trouble this little coyote pup would be causing as he grew each day!

Ultimately, the youngsters decided to bring their parents into their secret. This was necessary, they reasoned, because they knew whatever the parents decided would have to be obeyed.

Both Andrew and Haven got little sleep the night before they were to talk to their parents.

It would be easiest to have the discussion at the breakfast table, they decided. [Everyone must face hard decisions, and this was one of the hardest moments of their young lives.]

They had prepared for this moment like a trial lawyer would prepare for a trial. They had outlined their comments and practiced their presentation before this eventful breakfast. Andrew was becoming more and more like his attorney grandfather. He loved the research, law, and the excitement of protecting those who could not protect themselves.

Andrew began the discussion, and he recited the facts just as they occurred. He then related the law of Montana concerning the fate of wild animal babies who are orphaned.

He went on to explain the reason for their initial silence and secrecy. "We were both frightened for the coyote," he said. "It was important to act immediately to save the coyote pup, so we had to use only our own judgment." Both parents listened with great interest and did not interrupt Andrew. They were impressed with his research and presentation.

Haven was to have spoken next, but this was not possible because she was in the arms of her mother crying her eyes out! So, the case rested only on Andrew's words. Both youths knew Bandit's fate was now in the hands of their parents They determined to be still and wait for the decisions to be made. They knew they would not disobey them no matter what their decisions were going to be.

Haven continued crying with her arms wrapped around her mother. Even though she had practiced her presentation, she remained silent. But her actions spoke her argument better than words could have. Everyone in the room knew Haven's position on the matter. She was in love with her little Bandit just like her love for the kitty that had come into her life many years ago.

Her father asked her to explain how she was feeding and taking care of Bandit. She wiped the tears from her eyes, apologized, and then went into detail about the eye dropper, milk, and water from the same dropper, and how the hot water bottle was filled before leaving Bandit alone for the night.

She had placed an old wind-up clock in the box with him so the sound would keep him company when she was not there and at night.

Everyone was now ready for the big moment—the moment when their parents would react to the entire situation. But there was silence, which terrified the young students.

And then, breaking the silence, their father finally started to speak. Andrew and Haven hung on every word of their father.

"I appreciate all you have done for this baby wild coyote, Bandit, he said. "I agree it was an almost impossible situation. You remember when we took the little bear cub, Brownie Bear, to the vet when he had been attacked by the Mountain Lion? We did not think for a minute about taking him immediately to the vet to have him treated. He was not a pet bear, but he followed you and Haven around just like he was a pet. This situation is no different.

"Here is what we are going to do. Andrew and I will take Bandit to the animal hospital. I will ask the doctor to remain quiet about his treatment until we determine whether this little fellow will even make it."

Bandit was now the center of attention. Haven proudly showed how much this little pup was growing day by the day. His little teeth were sharp as razors. He was alert and limping around on the emergency stent which had been placed on his right front leg. He seemed to love and trust everyone who would give him attention.

So, Bandit went off to the animal hospital with Andrew and his understanding father.

Bandit had no idea what was in store for him; he was simply happy to have all this attention and the company of his friend Andrew.

He rode on Andrew's lap on his way to the hospital and stood up and looked out the window as the forest of Glacier Park passed them by.

"Well, this should be interesting, little Bandit," Andrew said to the pup. I am nervous about being here, but I know this is going to be alright. You will like this doctor; he saved a little bear cub we brought in after he was attacked by a Mountain Lion. That is a long story, but that little bear reminds me of you and the problems you have had."

Bandit paid no attention to Andrew. He was interested in watching the scenery and approaching buildings.

When they arrived at the animal hospital, the whole staff of doctors and assistants were there to see this pup coyote and to treat him as an emergency patient. Everyone went into action, which put the little coyote into the center of attention. He did not want to be! He was taken in by a nurse who smiled as she carried him.

Andrew and his father waited in the waiting room making small talk and watching others who had brought pets for treatment.

Time was going slowly, so Andrew started thinking about his next plan for his beloved little Bandit.

When the doctor came in, the entire waiting room watched! He was carrying a small pet cat carrier in one hand and his patient chart in the other hand. He called Andrew and his father into the office and sat down with them to go over the exam.

Bandit had his nose outside of the crate and was yapping. Then he started to make a small howl.

Andrew calmed him, "Hey fellow! Quiet down! Everyone can hear you."

The vet was polite and came right to the point. He said the pup was dehydrated and would need an IV to get him up to normal, so they hooked him up to an IV. The pup also showed signs of needing more solid food, so the vet showed Andrew a document which explained the proper care and diet he and Haven should follow.

The doctor noted the right front leg was healing and the stent had worked. He was generally pleased with the care by the children. He handed Andrew a document showing all the necessary shots had been given as if the coyote was a pet dog. Rabies, distemper, and other shots would protect the pup and the public.

Bandit's food menu would change, and he would be getting some puppy food and some newly designed formula for better nutrition.

When the IV was finished, Andrew picked up the little pup, placed him in his new little crate, and they started home.

It seemed Bandit was ready to start barking and howling on a regular basis.

CHAPTER 4

THE 'GENIE' IS OUT OF THE BOTTLE

Life would never be the same at the Lodge. Andrew and Haven had unleashed a "genie" out of a magic lamp, and that little genie was starting to change everything around.

Bandit was getting bigger and braver.

He wanted to explore and leave immediately to go into the wild. But everyone knew he would not last one night on his own in the wild, so they had to keep a close eye on him

Out in the wilderness there were bobcats, foxes, raccoons, other coyotes, mountain lions and bears to contend with. Wolves could be heard howling. Andrew knew they were close. There was no doubt little Bandit would be in danger if he were in the wild on his own.

Glacier Haven was close to nature at its best with the wilderness of Glacier National Park on the north side of the road and a designated wilderness area on the other side.

Andrew and Haven knew they would have to watch Bandit closely to keep him calm and help him thrive in captivity.

Fortunately, everything was normal to Bandit. He did not know what life would be like in the wild.

One day, Andrew suggested to his sister, "How about if we call our grandfather and ask his advice?"

Papa Hanson was their mother's father. Andrew and his sister had hiked with him, fished with him, and even camped outside in the forest with him. Both were happy to have him around, and Andrew and Haven loved to work side by side with him at the resort. They knew a call to Papa, a retired trial lawyer, would help.

"Hi Papa! This is Andrew with Haven, and we have a question and need your help."

Their grandfather was always glad to hear from them.

He said, "I am so glad you called, and you sound like you are excited about something."

A description of the facts and details were given to their grandfather, who listened to every word and then had many questions to ask each of the grandchildren.

He said, "I really understand your problem, and this will take a lot of my time. I have not been in a Courtroom in the last ten years. But I will help you to the best of my ability. And I cannot wait to meet Bandit.

"I will call you back as soon as I have finished with some preliminary matters."

Again, the wait for Papa's call back weighed on their hearts.

"Well, Bandit," Andrew said to the pup while they waited, "you have caused more problems in a few weeks than Haven and I can remember."

Haven replied, "Don't be so hard on poor Bandit. He has not done anything wrong, and I know Papa will come up with some good ideas for saving him."

Fear and anxiety flared in Andrew's mind when he thought of the impossible legal problems which faced his family in defending Bandit.

In his mind this case was as important as a murder trial. Bandit risked being put down, and the pup had no idea he was even in danger.

Haven addressed Bandit, "Papa will protect you little Bandit, and I know he will help figure a way to save our precious little member of the family. He has always loved my kitty and I know he will love you."

Andrew found comfort in knowing Papa would be the one who would open a file and would begin his investigation into how to help Bandit.

A client who knew he could lose his life if he lost the Court case would find comfort in knowing someone was on his side and could skillfully advocate for him before a Judge.

But Bandit only found comfort in each moment. He had the attention span of a hummingbird and had no idea that his fate was hanging in the balance. Eating, drinking, barking, howling, and exploring were the only emotions apparent in this little coyote. He had, however, grown fond of a soccer ball. He rolled it in every direction. He also liked to sling a toy animal monkey into the air and then run to catch it. This independent play could go on for hours. He never slowed down until he collapsed from exhaustion. He would then sleep for hours.

Meanwhile, Andrew and Haven found comfort knowing Bandit's defense was in the hands of their hero, Papa, teacher, attorney, and advisor.

They knew Papa would do his best, and they knew little Bandit had a protector and defense attorney "money could not buy."

CHAPTER 5

LET THE INVESTIGATION BEGIN

When an attorney accepts a case, he opens a file to document facts, witnesses, law and regulations, a list of physical evidence, and statements of witnesses taken in the investigation.

This attorney (Papa) had tried cases to juries and Judges, across the state. He had argued in the Montana Supreme Court many times and seemed to be at home in the Courtroom.

It would be fair to say their Papa was happy in retirement and was reluctant to come out of retirement for any reason. But for Andrew and Haven, he would do anything.

The Montana Supreme Court approved his application to reactivate his membership in the Montana State Bar Association for the sole purpose of Bandit's case.

He sensed some of the justices would probably find it unusual, if not humorous, for him to go to all this time and trouble for an orphaned coyote pup. They knew Mr. Hanson had been a successful attorney. Why in the world would he come out of retirement for this matter?

Nonetheless, Papa went to work!

Montana regulations concerning orphaned rabies vectors such as foxes, raccoons and coyotes (by inclusion as a candidate) are quite clear:

"...If the animal cannot be returned (to the place it was found), it may have to be humanely euthanized. The center does not take animals considered rabies vectors, such as raccoons, bats, or foxes. Some raptors are accepted, but game species like geese and ducks are not. The center takes orphaned bears and mountain lions, under some circumstances...."

The R.V. Park had been full since early spring, keeping the young students busy every day. And most days, Andrew and Haven had to work overtime.

But at every free moment, they would care for Bandit. Days went by quickly.

For fun, they decided to try a game to give Bandit exercise.

Andrew suggested to Haven, "Let us see just how smart Bandit really is. You run and hide, and I will ask Bandit to follow your trail and find you."

So, Haven ran into the forest about five hundred yards and hid behind a giant spruce tree.

Andrew then released Bandit and encouraged him to follow Haven's trail. He did not need much help. Bandit immediately followed the trail and found Haven hiding without any trouble at all. She always had a treat for him, and then he stuck right by her side each time they finished the game.

It was a fun exercise. They continued the game, making it more difficult for Bandit each time. They took turns running and hiding. Then they came up with the idea that Bandit should be able to find a garment belonging to one of them. They put on heavy rubber boots to hide their own scent, and Andrew dragged an old sweatshirt of Haven's on the ground, leaving it behind a bush. Then he ran back to Haven and Bandit.

They turned Bandit free to find the sweatshirt if he could. It was hidden over 500 yards from Bandit. He was anxious to go! When released, he moved like lightning through the forest and straight to Haven's sweatshirt, which he brought back.

The experiment worked so well, they decided to use a sweatshirt of their father for Bandit to find. If he were successful, Bandit would prove himself as an accomplished tracker.

Bandit not only found the sweatshirt of their father, but he did it faster than he had ever done before. What a discovery; what a way to exercise the pup!

They could hardly wait to tell Papa about this test when they visited with him by phone that evening

"Papa!" Andrew said. "Bandit has now proven he is as good a tracker as a Bloodhound. We have given him mini tests to track not only people, but also to find pieces of clothing we have dragged on the ground and then hid behind trees or bushes.

"It is not only a fun game, but it will surely prove to the Judge that Bandit is a great coyote and could be as useful as a Bloodhound in search and rescue."

Papa was amused at the descriptions by Andrew. "Andrew," he said, "you have always had a great imagination and you and Haven are perfect people to be training young Bandit."

He went on, "I must say, however, the coming trial we're going to have will not be dependent upon how smart or how playful Bandit is, but rather will be dependent upon whether the Lodge would be a good place to rehabilitate the pup. In other words, we are going to have to prove Bandit will be safe.

"You must keep Bandit from the public, and you must keep the public away from Bandit. "Both of you, Andrew and Haven, will have to learn many lessons before we will be ready for trial."

They discussed a time when Papa could come to the resort and meet Bandit. A time was set, and the training continued.

What a smart and clever coyote Bandit had become.

CHAPTER 6

BANDIT MEETS HIS ATTORNEY

Papa came to the Lodge.

He was met by Andrew and Haven as he pulled into the main driveway, and, as expected Haven was holding the little coyote who was licking at her face.

What an exciting moment for them. Bandit was to meet Papa, and the day had great promise! Papa was there to give them hope and courage to carry on with their plan to save Bandit from a possible tragedy. Papa would try to keep the Montana Fish and Game agents from seizing precious Bandit and having him euthanized by virtue of its laws and regulations.

There was, however, no feeling on the part of Andrew, Haven, or Papa that the laws and regulations of the State of Montana were wrong or evil. They just hoped there might be a way they could keep this pup.

Papa said he believed there should be an exception granted to Bandit by the Court. He said that, because Bandit's mother had been accidentally killed by the train, the youth could not have put him back where they found him—it would have meant certain death!

Besides having a severely injured right front foot which needed immediate treatment, Bandit would have died from starvation and shock within hours if he had not been rescued.

Could there be an exception, then, in Bandit's case? Questions were racing through Haven's and Andrew's minds. Was there a chance for him; could they keep Bandit?

All Bandit wanted at that time was to be held by Papa. Papa gladly took him and patted him on the top of the head.

Because Papa was a stranger, Bandit had to get to know him. He sniffed his hand and gently bit him on the hands and fingers. Like all little animals, Bandit did not mean to hurt Papa, and Papa knew it.

Papa said, "Well, Bandit. We finally meet. You have caused more trouble and chaos around here than anything I can remember!

"You are going to have to get along with everyone in the family, including the family cat, and that relationship may be your biggest test."

Papa then did something quite unexpected. He got down on his hands and knees, set Bandit beside him, and yelled out a loud howl—the kind of howl all of us have heard when a coyote is howling at night.

Bandit shook his little head, pointed his nose up into the air and repeated back the most perfect howl the children had ever heard Bandit make. When Papa howled, Bandit howled. They howled again and again.

Papa was amused, and so were Andrew and Haven. What an unlikely sight: an old man and a baby coyote on the ground and both howling to the sky!

Andrew's Mother was just coming out of the Lodge and she saw her father on his hands and knees howling into the air and little Bandit with his nose pointed to the sky howling back.

She said, "What in the world is Papa doing?"

Haven replied with a smile on her face, "Papa is teaching Bandit to howl like a coyote."

Her mother simply smiled and went back into the Lodge.

Bandit learned to come when called and to sit, stay, and bark. Each time Bandit obeyed; he received a reward of dry puppy treat.

CHAPTER 7

BANDIT AND THE FAMILY CAT

Bandit also met "Merry," the family cat of 14 years, soon after Andrew and Haven brought him home.

The unlikely pair first met on the floor of Bandit's playhouse home. To say the least the meeting did not go so well at first. After all, the playhouse was Merry's domain, and she had a mind of her own.

Bandit, with a playful heart ran to "Merry" with the utmost good intentions.

Merry responded by curling her back, raising the hair on her neck, and hissing at the innocent little coyote baby. Bandit backed up and watched with fear.

Haven left them alone, hoping the meeting would not turn into an attack by Merry and a total disaster.

Merry moved closer to Bandit, and then Bandit backed up some more. He whined with fear.

All the sudden, as if by magic, Merry began to lick Bandit's head. He stood still in terror. After a few minutes, though, "the lion had lain down with the lamb."

Bandit started to nap next to this family kitty, and Merry started purring as she lay down on the rug in the playhouse.

This trial of getting along with Merry was as important as the one coming in the Courtroom. Bandit would be able to live in peace with the entire family since he made friends with Merry. The two became inseparable.

The cat came and left when she wanted, and every afternoon you could see them snuggled up together.

CHAPTER 8

MAY IT PLEASE THE COURT!

Papa did not wait long before filing a motion with the Court. He did not want word to get out about the students harboring Bandit. If that happened, Bandit was subject to seizure by a game Warden, and that could be the bitter end of the matter. The little coyote would probably face certain death.

Papa drove to Kalispell and filed a motion and petition with the District Court.

The petition set forth all the facts and requested the Court to grant a temporary restraining order which would:

1. Restrain the Montana Fish and Game, its agents, and Wardens from taking control of the orphan coyote pup named Bandit.
2. Allow Andrew and Haven to be caretakers and have care, custody, and control of Bandit until further order of this Court.

3. Allow the Montana Game Warden to enter on the premises of the Lodge and investigate how the little pup was doing and how he was being cared for.

On the day for the hearing, they all drove to Kalispell and entered the parking lot of the Courthouse. Neither Andrew nor Haven had been in a Courtroom. They were nervous about being there.

When they walked into the Courtroom, they saw attorneys, witnesses, and clients seated in the appropriate areas. The District Judge was sitting behind a large structure known as the Bench where she had enough room to write and make notes as she listened to the testimony.

The Montana Fish and Game was present, through their attorney and the local Fish and Game Warden.

Andrew and Haven were both up front sitting with Papa.

The Judge called the case for the hearing.

Papa spoke, "May it please the Court.

"This is the time set for the hearing to decide whether or not the Court should grant a temporary restraining order in favor of Andrew and Haven, restraining the Fish and Game from seizing a baby coyote pup that was saved by them when they discovered the pup near a railroad track by the premises of the Inn and Lodge where they are employed. Their parents own the Lodge and the petitioners are the children of the owners.

"This week-old baby coyote was barely living, and his mother had been killed by a passing train. The high school students reasoned the mother coyote was probably moving the pup by the nape of his neck when crossing the train track, and the train hit his mother and severely injured the pup. "I will refer to the pup coyote as 'Bandit' through the remaining proceedings.

"Andrew and Haven picked up Bandit and took him to a safe place. He was treated for the injuries he had suffered.

“Andrew and Haven researched medical treatment on a computer and found the coyote was probably in shock.

“Haven ran to get a hot water bottle filled with warm water and some small blankets.

“Andrew, at the same time, hurried to get the family first aid kit and started preparing fine strips of tape so he could engineer a small stick splint for the pup’s right front leg.

“He applied the stent and laid the baby coyote on a blanket. A hot water bottle served as a gentle heater under the blanket.

“Haven proceeded to figure out how to feed him.

“She decided to make a formula from cream, milk, and a bit of honey. She used an eyedropper to feed Bandit. She fed this precious milk potion to him one drop at a time.

“Bandit enjoyed the attention and the life-giving milk. He slept in his little den made of a cardboard box, a hot water bottle, towels, and blankets.

“Andrew then researched what the law of Montana required.

“He knew it was necessary to give notice of the little coyote orphan to the Fish and Game service.

“He discovered he would no doubt be put down.

“A baby coyote would not be a good candidate for rehabilitation in a recognized and approved rehabilitation center. He would be considered a rabies vector and would probably be euthanized by the Fish and Game upon discovery.

“Their father decided Bandit should go to the Animal Hospital immediately and be examined and treated by a vet.

“Andrew and his father loaded up little Bandit and off they went to the vet. The vet gave the animal all the shots which a puppy would be given, including rabies distemper and tetanus. He was given an I.V. for severe dehydration and was examined for all the injuries he suffered in this violent train injury.

“To make a long story short, your Honor, the vet was pleased with Andrew’s treatment of the right front leg and his sister’s ability to figure out a formula which would keep the baby coyote alive.

"Part of the vet's written instructions included puppy food which came in small pieces that would not only exercise the mouth and teeth, but also would contain desperately needed nourishment.

"The vet suggested the children feed him using the food in a dog dish. He noted this dry food would be a perfect treat for training a dog or, in this case, training a baby coyote.

"After they visited the vet, they took the pup back to the playhouse that contained room for a table and chair, toys and a ladder, and a loft where a child could sit or take a nap. They are keeping Bandit at the playhouse at the present time. It is filled with all types of toys which keep Bandit busy.

"Andrew put in a doggie door so the little coyote could go in and out when he wanted to. He also built a sturdy fence around the playhouse to contain Bandit when he went out of the playhouse during the day. They made a self-filling watering dish and provided a dish for hard puppy food.

"The vet had stated it would be necessary to continue to feed Bandit with the eyedropper and specified the time when Haven could start weaning him and allow him to eat other food such as raw hamburger and pieces of sirloin steak.

"The vet insisted these children and their parents report this animal to the Montana Fish and Game Department as soon as they could, regardless of the consequences.

"Knowing this matter could be complicated and knowing it was a matter of life and death to Bandit, the children decided to call Papa.

"Your Honor, I am a retired Montana attorney who practiced in this state for 40 years and have been a member of the Montana State Bar Association for the last 50 years.

"I have been reinstated to an active status as a member of the Montana Bar Association solely for the purpose of trying this case to the Court.

"I have met Bandit, and he is safely at home at the Lodge."

"I told both Andrew and Haven this case is unusual because the rules of the Fish and Game are there to help and protect our wildlife.

"To succeed in this case, I submit the Court can only consider what is best for the State of Montana and what is best for this innocent coyote baby.

"Fortunately, these two young students have worked and lived at the Inn owned by their parents since they were four and six years old. So, they are familiar with the area.

"They hiked and bicycled in the area all their lives and worked almost every day, helping their parents during the summer. They have had to deal with wild animals frequently. They would be most qualified to raise this orphan coyote.

"For example, several years ago, these young students rescued a tiny black bear cub who had been savagely attacked by a mountain lion near Glacier Haven Inn.

"They immediately took the baby bear to the same vet who treated Bandit, and he was able to save the bear.

"Both had to physically rehabilitate the bear over several weeks before it could be returned to the wild forest.

"And when that day came, the bear was able to walk and eat without help. So, they took the bear to the edge of the forest by their property and released him. It returned to its mother.

"Later, the cub was spotted at his mother's side near the Lodge. They witnessed this little bear adapted properly and was truly a wild animal again!

"I know the case before the Court concerning Bandit is far different than the bear cub case.

"But the Court should take into consideration that, even if Bandit completely survives this traumatic accident that killed his mother, he would never be able to be released back into the wild as a self-sustaining wild animal.

"Consequently, the question before the Court is whether these young high school students can rehabilitate and manage to raise

Bandit in an environment which is both safe to Bandit and safe to the public.

"I bring before the Court an emotional and almost impossible question: "Should Bandit live or should Bandit be turned over to the Fish and Game Warden to be dealt with according to their regulations, which would mean almost certain death.

"Your Honor, I would ask the Court to issue the restraining order pending its final ruling in this matter.

"I have filed with the Court an affidavit signed by both Andrew and Haven where they meticulously set out exactly all the facts which I have given you in this argument.

"Should the Court want to hear their testimony, they are present in the Courtroom.

"Your Honor, we would ask this Court to consider equity as well as the rules of law. This case requires mercy and equity.

"I have filed, with the Court, a proposed order.

"Thank You."

The Fish and Game attorney then stood up and acknowledged this was a serious problem.

He related to the Court that, oftentimes a person will think a fawn or baby elk, bear or even a coyote has been abandoned when, in fact, they have not been. They simply have been left in place by the mother.

He stated, "The rule of the woods and in Montana, is quite simple: if you find a baby animal in the woods, leave it and move on."

The Attorney went on to say, "I acknowledge, in this case, there are facts and circumstances which may call for a different response by the person coming across this situation. What young person is going to leave an orphan coyote in the woods when its mother has been killed by a moving train?

"The State of Montana is not anxious to decide to put down this pup without giving the matter a great deal of thought.

"Your Honor, at this time, we will not object to the temporary order. I would like to visit the premises, and make suggestions on the type of care, shelter and food which may be helpful to the caretakers. The ultimate position of the State will be set forth within 60 days."

The Judge did not hesitate. She stated, "I will grant the TRO (temporary restraining order) and set this matter for hearing two months from now. If there is no further business, Court will be adjourned."

Andrew and Haven were happy and relieved. Bandit was safe at least for 60 days!

They all headed home to the Lodge at Glacier Park.

Meanwhile at the Lodge, Bandit had no idea what was keeping Haven from the feeding schedule, but he was playing with Merry the cat and would soon fall to sleep.

Everyone sat down to the dinner Papa's daughter had prepared—Papa's favorite—pot roast, potatoes, salad, and apple pie.

Bandit was in his travel crate furnished by the animal hospital. He was sound asleep, but present at the dinner.

Everyone talked about the Court hearing and what had happened.

Haven was impressed by the formality of the Courtroom, and she was surprised the District Judge was a woman.

CHAPTER 9

THE CAT IS OUT OF THE BAG

Papa was tired, but he had a new attitude about his life. He enjoyed getting back into the law for this case. He enjoyed the research, the investigation, the action of the Court procedure and the opportunity to serve and help his clients.

It was even more special to serve Andrew, Haven and Bandit. After all, it was Papa who taught Bandit to "howl like a coyote."

When you are retired and getting older, one of the disappointments of your life is that much of your talent is not being used each day.

For example, putting in new furnace filters, watering plants and helping with grocery shopping seems to take more time and is far less challenging than endeavors such as speaking in Court, writing briefs, and working on a legal case. The other thing he missed was fly fishing.

Papa's work was now law, if only for a moment in time, and he appeared to have a "spring" in his step. He loved his new purpose.

Papa did not notice the minor aches and pains of his body. He did not even give a thought as to how tired he had become by nightfall after researching all day how to raise a wild coyote puppy to adulthood.

The internet provided interesting life examples of people who had raised foxes, coyotes and wolves found as puppies. Most found it was impossible…some succeeded.

On the political front he contacted others for helpful hints and those who were politically connected with the Governor of Montana if Papa lost this legal fight and the Court would order the tiny coyote be euthanized by the Fish and Game.

Andrew and Haven also were faced with new problems. Bandit was taking too much time. They had to watch, feed, nurture and exercise the pup each day.

Bandit was growing up. He was thriving and growing in stature.

Oh, if only Bandit was a normal puppy, life would be so much easier. The extra duties demanded by Bandit seemed insurmountable.

Merry the cat, friend, and companion of Bandit, was a perfect babysitter. But Bandit knew he had to be careful because Merry would not hesitate to hit him with a paw and knock him completely over if he crossed her the wrong way.

She was with him for hours each day and they were truly inseparable. This was good for Bandit because he had a friend and companion when Andrew and Haven had to work. Merry was probably a better protector than anyone. As far as Andrew was concerned, Merry may now have more to do with Bandit's care than anyone.

While Papa was still at the resort, his favorite pastime was to take the little coyote for long walks. The walks were good for both.

Time flew by at the Lodge, and Papa seemed to enjoy his time he was able to spend there.

He enjoyed a video he had found on "You Tube" of a woman in England who took in baby foxes and helped them until it was time to return to the wild.

Her experience was interesting to watch because the fox pups were active and difficult to control.

After six months, she found the foxes would go through what she called the "crazies," and they would become impossible to control.

This was the time she would release the baby foxes into the wild again. Of course, England was different from Montana, and coyotes were different from foxes.

Eventually, Papa left Glacier Park and returned to his retirement home in Arizona.

There he made his office the center of his attention. Between legal research, outlining strategy, and talking with officials, he was busy.

In Papa's mind, this was like the good old days except he was working from home instead of an office and only had one case. What a luxury to have so much time to work on this important matter.

He had become a happy, busy attorney with a purpose to serve his clients, Andrew, Haven, and little Bandit. Everyone knew he was spending too much time on this case, but that is what he had—time.

When his personal friends and even strangers heard about this case, they encouraged him and his grandchildren at Glacier Park.

The newspaper in Kalispell had picked up the story of the orphaned coyote, and an unexpected flood of support by people in the Kalispell area developed.

"The cat is out of the bag," Papa stated to his grandchildren as the news spread across the state.

Animal lovers were coming to Bandit's side. America is a country of free speech, Papa thought, but this media attention could have unintended consequences.

The Montana Fish and Game was not happy with all the publicity. Not that it was anyone's fault. But the publicity was putting into question one of the milestone regulations in the Fish and Game's quiver of arrows.

In other words, they did not want this case to interfere with their day-to-day operations. The public was already interfering with the baby wild animals found alone in the wild. They would show up with a fawn or a baby bear and tell the Ranger it was abandoned.

Also, he was sure there were cases where people tried to raise wild baby animals and failed.

This was important because if Bandit got away and did not come back, it would leave hope in Andrew and Haven's mind that the coyote went back into the wild without a problem. The law, however, had no exceptions:

Leave a baby fawn, cub, or pup when you come across it in the wild. Do not forget the mother animal is near and will properly take care of its little one. Do not pick it up and take it to the game Warden or to the Fish and Game office.

Do not try to sneak and raise the baby yourself. All the efforts of the public when they do not follow the rules, end in disaster. No exceptions!

Another reason Papa was not happy about all the publicity was because the District Court Judge's decision had to be according to the law of Montana, regardless of the public support for Bandit.

Papa wondered if the Fish and Game would object to the plan by Andrew and Haven, just to make an example.

CHAPTER 10

AN UNSPEAKABLE CRIME

If the matters around Glacier Haven Inn were not busy enough, something then occurred that terrified the community.

A young man found along the Going to the Sun Highway had been severely injured, seemed to have been beaten, and had incurred a severe blow to the head. His girlfriend had been kidnapped at the same time he was attacked.

Ambulance drivers arrived and immediately tried to rehabilitate this young man. He was still breathing.

Law enforcement arrived. The Glacier Park Rangers were trained to act. The first thing they did was to search the young man's car. Unfortunately, they found nothing which would raise any suspicion he had done anything to deserve the beating.

The ambulance care workers administered oxygen and were treating the young man for shock. He was coming around. He was resuscitated enough for law enforcement Rangers to talk to him.

He opened his eyes and saw the EMT workers and two Glacier National Park law enforcement officers. He kept asking where Holly, his girlfriend, had gone. He told them his name was Tony and could remember only that they were walking along Lake McDonald when two young men stopped and talked with them.

Tony recovered enough from his injuries to be able to sit up in the ambulance. He was bleeding badly from his head injury and had been savagely beaten, but he knew he had to live to help his dear Holly who had been kidnapped by these men.

Tony said the men stopped and asked, "Hey how are you guys? We are looking around and thought you could help. We wonder if you can give us some information about the area."

Tony said he and Holly were friendly and replied, "We are new to the Park and this is as far as we have come on this highway. We don't really know what is ahead."

The men then started acting strangely. They said they just wondered where they could stop, have lunch, and then take a hike.

Tony said they started to get awfully close to them, and suddenly one grabbed Tony while the other grabbed Holly and started to drag her to his car. Both were strong and fought back violently.

One of the kidnappers then grabbed a large rock and hit Tony on the head. Tony fought back, but everything stopped suddenly when Tony was hit in the face with the rock. Tony went down and started to lose consciousness; they left Tony for dead.

Even though he was almost unconscious, Tony could hear Holly screaming. Nonetheless, he lay still and played like he was dead.

He knew he could help Holly more by acting as though he were dead than he could by trying to get up.

He was discovered by a tourist who went to West Glacier Station to report the injured Tony and led the emergency ambulance workers to Tony.

A call for help to find Holly went out to all law enforcement officers in the area. The emergency "all hands-on deck" gave instructions to proceed to Lake McDonald, and to keep the call confidential. The last thing law officers needed was a member of the public trying to help outside of the control of Rangers in Glacier Park.

Hikers and tourists were ordered to leave the Park immediately, and all persons leaving were questioned and cleared by law officers when they departed at the ports of entry. All employees of the Park and the concessions were ordered to stay in place.

Outside law officers started to enter the Park to start the search for the kidnappers and for young Holly who was no doubt terrified and was in grave danger.

In addition to Park Rangers, there were Montana Highway Patrol officers, deputy sheriffs from Kalispell, and Forest Service law enforcement officers. Also, all the Fish and Game Wardens were called to duty.

Helicopters took off with law enforcement officers aboard. The Park Service moved Ranges and horses to the area where they found the injured young man.

All law enforcement officers were heavily armed and would be able to travel across the Park at a fast pace, including Park Rangers on horseback and law enforcement in helicopters and squad cars.

At the time the news broke to law officers about the kidnapping, a Fish and Game Warden just happened to be at the Glacier Haven Inn premises meeting with Andrew.

Andrew had just informed the Warden about the exercise of having Bandit follow a scent left on the ground by a person trying to hide. Andrew had told him Bandit was better at tracking people than a Bloodhound!

When the Warden got the notice to help in the search and rescue, he had an idea! Why not take Andrew and Bandit into the wild with him and let Bandit attempt to track the young lady who had been kidnapped. They could use her clothing that had been left in Tony's car as scent to start the search. Once he smelled the clothing of Holly, Bandit would know they were going to play the game he had learned so well. He would track and find Holly!

Andrew was also an experienced hiker and had explored the trails and wilderness in the area which would be searched.

It was a long shot, but the Warden got permission by the law enforcement leadership to proceed with this attempt to track the kidnappers. In fact, the mix of law enforcement agents were quite excited in having an expert hiker and his coyote tracker to help them.

Before they left the Lodge, Andrew packed a backpack with all the essential items for overnight camping—parkas, compass, knife, mess kit, cups, dried back-packing food, a goose down vest, jacket, and a sleeping bag. He also packed lights which fit on his forehead for night hiking, one for him and one for the Warden.

Andrew knew he could be in the forest for a long time and brought what he thought would be needed, including a tarp, rope, fire starting candles, matches, and other necessities which would save a life. The pack contained a package of twelve "fun size" Snickers candy bars. This would be a treat when they needed energy. Also, he put into the backpack a supply of food for Bandit.

They proceeded with Andrew as a tracker and Bandit as a "Bloodhound."

The Warden, Andrew and Bandit boarded a helicopter sent directly to the Lodge. The experienced pilot was told where to fly and took them to the temporary headquarters on the highway near Lake McDonald.

CHAPTER 11

THE GAME BEGINS!

Andrew and the Warden were briefed by the Park Ranger in charge. Andrew was asked for his opinion about the matter; then he went to pick up some clothing Holly had been wearing earlier in the day.

Andrew also wanted to visit with Tony who was still in the ambulance. He did not want to leave without talking to the young man. The Ranger had told Tony that Andrew was going to try to track Holly with an unlikely partner, his coyote. The young coyote was to be used as a "Bloodhound." Andrew had some questions for Tony before they headed out. He asked about any clue that would help him in his search for the young man's girlfriend. He was looking for clues of where to start. The injured young Tony related something he just remembered.

He said that one of the two kidnappers yelled, "We have to get out of here in a hurry. This highway will be swarming with police. The sooner we get off this highway and onto a trail, the better off we will be."

That clue told Andrew they should start the search in the parking lot of Avalanche Lake trail. He reasoned these criminals would want to take the first turnoff with a trail to get off the Going to the Sun highway.

The Avalanche Lake trail had a large sign on the highway and would appeal to the kidnappers. It was a long shot, but, in his judgment, would be where he wanted to start. The Ranger agreed. "This young man, Andrew, seems to know the Park as well as we do."

The kidnappers may have left their car in the parking lot there, and it was the only trail into the Park for many miles. The Chief Ranger ordered the helicopter pilot to take Andrew, the Warden and Bandit to the parking lot at Avalanche Lake trail.

The helicopter landed and they noticed a car in the parking lot. It was unusual since the Park Ranger had ordered all persons to leave the Park. Someone might still be on the trail.

Bandit was given the young lady's clothing to smell. He sniffed the shirt and knew immediately he was going to play the game he had played so many times before. He could not wait to get started! He was then harnessed with a dog lead and proceeded to the trail. Andrew knew it would take no time at all to learn if he was right about this trail. If he were wrong, they would keep going to other trails on the way up the highway.

But as far as Andrew was concerned, the car in the Parking lot was another clue to the mystery of where the kidnappers were located. The question Andrew asked himself was, "Where would I go if I was trying to flee?" He was certain this spot would be a perfect choice.

They would know soon enough. If Bandit were on scent, Andrew would know it and, if not, they could start over at another location. They began walking down this beautiful trail which led into the heart of the south part of the Park. As they walked, Andrew felt Bandit move in a strange way. He was pulling so hard on the leash Andrew had to double the leather around his hand so Bandit could not get away!

The Warden alerted headquarters of the presence of the car. He did not know if he needed a search warrant, so they left the car and proceeded to the Avalanche Lake Trail.

After a short time, Andrew told the Warden he was sure Bandit was on scent. He continued holding Bandit back by the leash.

Andrew knew Bandit would find the girl whose clothing he had sniffed! The Warden was more skeptical about this whole affair. After all, the entire experiment was a long shot. He believed this mystery was not going to be solved easily or without possible heartache. After all, he was a lawman who had a lot of experience in investigating crime, and he only hoped they were on to the right trail. It was a matter of life and death.

Andrew repeated to the Warden, "I am sure Bandit is on the scent. I have done this so many times, and for some reason he has never failed to succeed when we played this game. Bandit will find the young lady by following the scent of the clothing, I'm sure!" They soon reached Avalanche Lake which was only a two-mile hike. It was the end of the trail.

Andrew said, "Sir, Bandit is still on track. I know he is on a fresh trail of Holly."

So, they proceeded into the woods without a trail to follow. They instead were led by this young coyote who did not seem to tire at all.

It was necessary to alert the nerve center of law enforcement that they had reached the end of the trail and were continuing.

"Calling Eagles Nest! Calling Eagles nest!" the Warden signaled.

"This is Eagle One! This is Eagle One! We think we are on the trail of the victim. We are at the foot of Avalanche Lake. We will proceed due south into the Park. No trail to follow; no trail to follow. Alert helicopters, planes, and Rangers on horseback of our location. Over."

Headquarters to Eagle's Nest, "10-4 Eagle One. Read you loud and clear. I will proceed with notices to helicopters, planes, and

Rangers. We will try to follow you by air. Stay in touch; Over and out."

Andrew had no trail to follow so he had to go around fallen trees, through brush and log jams. And because he was holding Bandit on a leash, he had to half walk and half run through the woods.

Fortunately, he was in great shape! The Warden was right behind him and kept up with no problem. He was older but was in great shape as well and was armed with a revolver and an automatic rifle with a powerful scope.

Andrew was unarmed.

Both were practically running at times when the brush was light. Bandit was on scent and they knew he was following a trail left by this precious young woman, Holly. They hoped she was still alive.

The law enforcement agents on horseback had reached Avalanche Lake but when they lost the trail, they could not keep up with Andrew and the Warden.

The dense forest made it hard to travel by foot, and on horseback it was almost impossible. So, Rangers on horseback stayed in contact with the Warden by radio.

Also, aircraft was following the Warden to search ahead to see if they could see from the air any trace of the criminal fugitives and Holly.

Currently, they were trusting in Bandit completely. Andrew was confident they were getting closer because Bandit was getting more and more eager to run ahead. It was a good thing the leash was heavy duty because it was getting a workout.

The sky was clear, but clouds started to build in Glacier Park. This could make things more difficult.

The mountains were so beautiful, and the clouds would be welcome at any other time, but Andrew knew rain could affect the scent on the trail. If the scent were diminished, that could lead to tragedy! They had to move faster to beat a possible storm!

Even though the criminals had a head start on the Warden and Andrew, the fast pace they were keeping, hour by hour, convinced Andrew they were gaining on the men.

Andrew said a prayer while he was walking. He had never experienced such emotional trauma at any time in his life.

Bandit, on the other hand, was simply playing his game and had no idea how important this exercise would be! The sun was starting to set.

Nightfall came, and after a brief break for food and water, the unlikely three would proceed into the night with the head lamps shining ahead on the trail. Both the Warden and Andrew were getting tired. Suddenly something was happening with Bandit!

CHAPTER 12

A CAT AND TWO MICE

Bandit was acting differently on the leash; he had slowed way down and the hair on his back was standing straight up. Andrew held up his hand, and he and the Warden got down on their knees. They crawled along the ground, staying as low as they could. There it was—the best news of the day. Something was bright and shiny ahead. A campfire.

Fortunately, Bandit was silent. A Bloodhound would be barking, but Bandit was completely silent and seemed to sense whoever was ahead was dangerous.

They could see a campfire with two men standing at the fire and a young woman tied to a nearby tree with a gag around her face.

The Warden signaled to Andrew to get behind him. They turned off their head lights. Bandit reminded Andrew of a cat sneaking up on a mouse. Bandit needed to be tied to tree. Andrew knew Bandit would not like being tied up and hoped he would not cry out or bark when they began sneaking up to the criminals. The Warden had the rifle with the scope covers off.

Andrew was unarmed but had a hunting knife on his belt in case he needed it. He also had a hardwood walking stick to protect him if needed.

The Warden whispered to Andrew to follow him on hands and knees.

Bandit was trying to get loose from the tree, but he was securely tied up.

The sneak was difficult. Andrew was frightened. He had never been in such a life and death situation.

Andrew knew the Warden would warn the criminals to raise their hands!

He doubted the criminals would give up.

The campfire illuminated everything. They could see both criminals and Holly. He also knew the Warden would shoot if they tried to do anything not in accordance with his exact instructions.

The Warden yelled out, "Put your hands in the air! This is the law and you are under arrest!"

One criminal made a run for his rifle which was up against a tree. The Warden shot twice, and the criminal fell to the ground. He was hit, and Andrew wondered if he was dead.

The other criminal then raised his hands in the air and yelled, "Don't shoot!"

Andrew helped put hand cuffs on both criminals (even though one of them was unconscious from the gun shot). Andrew could see the outlaw was shot in the right leg. The Warden was a crack shot and with the scope he could shoot to kill or shoot to wound. In this case the criminal was lucky to be alive, even though he was severely injured.

The young Holly, tied to the tree, was trying to talk. Andrew quickly untied her and took off the gag. He then held the young lady and asked her if she was alright.

The young lady whimpered, "I think I am alright, and thank you for finding me." She then started to cry.

Andrew said, "I am Andrew and I have been assisting the Game Warden to find you."

Andrew went on, "I will be right back. I have someone I want you to meet."

He returned with Bandit who was instantly in love with Holly, recognizing her from the scent of her clothes. He climbed right into her lap, licked her face, and snuggled into her arms. What an ice breaker for Bandit. He won her heart!

Evidently, he was proud to have found this young lady who had played the game with him!

Bandit had no idea how much trauma this young lady had gone through, but he made a perfect companion to a person who was rescued.

Andrew avoided talking about what had happened to Tony.

Instead, he said, "You can thank Bandit for finding you. No one could have tracked these men through the forest and brush without him."

He went on, "This is a long story, but while we are waiting for the rescue crew, let me tell you as much as I can."

He went on to tell Holly about his sister and how they found Bandit as a tiny baby who had lost his mother. From there, he related about the medical care, the visit to the vet and the Court hearing.

He told her of the little game of teaching Bandit to follow a trail. It was a fun game and the game that eventually was the one which saved her life. Evidently, a coyote's sense of smell is so great it can follow a trail better than any Bloodhound.

Andrew then reached into his backpack and took out a Snickers bar. He handed it to the young woman with a smile. She was starved, and the candy was just what she needed. Then he reached into the pack to find the goose down jacket and placed it around her shoulders.

She was in shock and she held onto Bandit who seemed to be a great comfort to her.

What a sight, what a miracle. This young coyote had tracked this young lady—by scent—through many miles of terrain without a trail and without professional training.

It was more than three hours before the rescue team reached them. They had come on horseback, but they decided not to take her out on horseback at night. They pinpointed their exact location with headquarters and stated they wanted a large helicopter brought in at daybreak.

Around the campfire the Warden told Andrew law enforcement is trained to shoot to kill when they decided to shoot at a criminal. The Warden stated, "In this case I shot at his right leg to stop him but hopefully not to kill him. He is a young man and I did not want to kill him. I am glad the other man surrendered. The Courts will work all of this out."

Unfortunately, Andrew did not have enough medical gear to handle the critical medical case of the kidnapper who had been shot. He did the best he could to stabilize the outlaw. He was able to stop the bleeding in his right leg.

The criminals remained in handcuffs and leg chains and waited for the helicopter along with everyone else.

Anyway you look at it, Bandit, the Warden, and Andrew were heroes and saved this young woman's life. The cat (Bandit) found the two mice.

The next morning, when the helicopter arrived, law enforcement officers loaded passengers and took the criminal who had been injured to the Kalispell hospital. The other criminal was taken by the sheriff to jail.

Holly was taken to the hospital as well. She had Bandit in her lap during the ride and kissed him on the forehead and thanked him for saving her life. She held on to him until they arrived at the entrance to the emergency room where she had to relinquish him to Andrew.

Andrew handed her another Snickers candy and said goodbye.

The young lady was treated and examined for injuries and mental health. She was placed in a room adjacent to her boyfriend, Tony, who was being treated for severe head injuries.

She was able to visit Tony and encourage him as he healed from the injuries he suffered.

The Warden and Andrew were cheered by a small group which gathered around the hospital.

All the TV newscasters were on hand requesting interviews, which were politely refused. The Warden and Andrew proceeded to the Fish and Game office to give detailed reports to law enforcement and agency management.

Bandit simply followed along on his leash. He was given puppy treats and water as they travelled from one location to the other. Andrew kept him close and petted him on top of his head.

Andrew knew little Bandit was the true hero, and without him, the young lady would never have been found so quickly and probably would not have been found alive.

CHAPTER 13

BACK TO COURT

So, the family, including Bandit, headed back to Court.

And there was Papa again, standing before the Judge.

"May it please the Court," he said.

"Your Honor. Now is the time set for hearing on the temporary restraining order you issued concerning this matter of the orphan coyote.

"I will make this brief. Nearly all the progress of this orphan pup coyote has been placed in the report which was filed with the Court.

"As you have probably read in the newspapers, our Bandit is now a hero."

The Courtroom was crowded with curious townspeople who had come to hear how this matter would end.

The tension and silence were prevalent. All could hear a pin drop.

The District Judge stated, "This has truly been a very emotional case, and I appreciate all of the legal work you have done. Is the Fish and Game ready for argument? The attorney for the Fish and Game

Department stood and told the Judge they were ready to proceed. The attorney stated, "Your Honor, this story is almost unbelievable. This coyote pup has saved a life and has proven he is able to live with Andrew and Haven without further supervision.

"The Director of the Fish and Game wanted me to convey his agreement that care, custody and control of Bandit would be granted to Andrew and Haven.

CHAPTER 14

A NEWS CONFERENCE

It is hard to put everything that had happened in a "nutshell" or end it with a simple ceremony. But a news conference would be a good start to put everything that happened to rest. Tony and Holly would not be in the news conference, but they were in the audience.

Many of the law enforcement officers were there. Even Bandit, in his trainer's arm, was present.

The Warden was asked to say a few words. He was thankful for the outcome and thanked every person involved in the rescue.

The Warden thanked the small coyote pup, Bandit, and Andrew, his trainer. He briefly explained Bandit was an orphan coyote whose mother was killed by a train. Andrew and Haven had raised him and trained him up to this point of time. Bandit was alert and wanted out of Andrew's arm.

The Warden concluded by saying the Coyote would be granted permanent custody to Andrew and Haven.

Papa was so proud of Andrew, Haven, and dear Bandit. Later there would be a dinner at the Lodge to celebrate this wonderful news.

Andrew and Haven's mother summed it up perfectly when she said, "If you had asked me whether you could have a puppy, I would have said no! But we are all delighted with Bandit. We love the cat; we love the coyote pup! We should all give thanks he was able to find Holly and save her life."

Papa returned home the next day. He and his wife would come to visit quite often. Of course, Bandit and the kitty would look forward to seeing both.

The coyote stayed close to the students. He never attempted to return to the wild. The cat and the coyote were inseparable. Bandit never knew he was a wild animal. He was raised by two high school students and a cat.

Made in the USA
Monee, IL
27 June 2023